By Jennifer Gray ★ Illustr...

The Travels of ERMINE
(who is very determined)

Trouble in New York

Dear Michael,

I am writing to tell you that I have recently adopted a very determined young lady named Ermine and I am sending her on a trip to see the world. New York City seems like a good place to start, so I have given her your address and told her to look you up. I am sure you will take care of her and show her the sights. She will be arriving next Wednesday afternoon.

Please send my regards to the former Mrs Megabucks and say hello to Mike Junior for me.

With best wishes,

Maria Grand Duchess Maria Von Schnitzel

Michael S Megabucks

Megabucks Bank

Wall Street

Manhattan

New York City

United States of America

Chapter 1

Manhattan, NYC...

Michael S Megabucks sat at his mega-desk in his mega-office drinking a mega-cup of coffee. The office was at the top of a mega-building overlooking the mega-skyline of Manhattan in New York City.

Megabucks House was one of the tallest skyscrapers in the city and the bird's-eye view of the glittering glass buildings was spectacular, especially in the winter sunshine. Michael S Megabucks never tired of it.

He swivelled round and round in his leather chair to take another look.

"Excuse me, Mr Megabucks." His assistant poked his head round the door.

"Whadisit, Sam?" Michael S Megabucks scowled.

"There's someone here to see you, Sir."

"I thought I told ya to keep this afternoon free." Michael S Megabucks had one son – Mike Junior. Today was Mike Junior's eighth birthday and he had something special planned.

"I'm real sorry, Sir," said the assistant, running his fingers through his hair. "I've told her to come back tomorrow but she just won't take no for an answer. She says you're expecting her." He raised his eyebrows.

"Something about a postcard…from a duchess?"

"Oh, shoot!" Michael S Megabucks said. "I'd forgotten all about that. You'd better send the young lady in."

"Thank you, Sir."

Michael S Megabucks heard a scampering sound on the corridor's marble floor. "Hey!" he yelled after the assistant. "Did she bring a dog?"

"No, Sir," the assistant called. "She's on her own."

"What's that scratching noise then?"

The assistant didn't reply. Instead he popped his head back round the mega-door and announced, "Miss Ermine, Sir."

A small, snow-white, furry animal with a long bushy tail, two coal-black eyes, white

9

whiskers and a pink nose trotted into the room. She was wearing a blue pinafore dress and a woolly scarf, and stood about half as high as his knee. A camera was slung over her shoulder and in one paw she carried a small bag marked TOOL KIT. She leaped up onto the desk.

"Hello," she said, "you must be Mike Senior." She removed a tatty photograph from her dress pocket and regarded him closely. "Although you're rather *different* from what I was expecting."

Michael S Megabucks blushed.

He and the Duchess were old friends. It was some time since he'd seen her, but he didn't think he'd changed *that* much. "*You're* Ermine?" he said, looking at her doubtfully. "Maria didn't say anything about a *weasel*."

Ermine gave him a frosty look. Her whiskers twitched. "I am NOT a weasel!" she said sternly. "I'm a stoat."

"What's the difference?" Michael S
Megabucks said.

"*What's the difference?*" Ermine spluttered.
"I turn white in the winter and brown in the
summer, for one. And I have a black tip on the
end of my tail –" she waved it in his direction
so he could see – "and I'm far cleverer. I live a
lot longer too, so I've got
lots and lots and *lots* of
relatives."

Michael S Megabucks
decided to change
the subject.

He didn't want the whole of Ermine's family descending on him from Balaclavia. "How d'ya come to know Maria?" he asked instead.

"The Duke wanted to use me to trim the collar of his robe," Ermine explained. "You know – the one he wore in the old days when he went to see the King."

"Ah," said Michael S Megabucks. He was dimly aware that Balaclavia no longer had a king and as a result the Duke and Duchess had fallen on hard times.

"The Duke still uses it for dressing up," Ermine told him. "He keeps it in a trunk at the castle, only the fur collar went mouldy because the castle roof was leaking. The Duchess told him to replace it with velvet instead but he set a trap to catch me anyway.

It's very precious, you know – my white fur. It's called ermine, like me." She let out a deep, shuddering sigh. "Can you believe that some people want to sew it onto *clothes*?"

"That sucks," Michael S Megabucks agreed.

"Luckily the Duchess came to the rescue," Ermine continued. "She told the Duke that the only place for ermine is on a stoat. Then she adopted me. She's taught me lots of useful things, like how to use a spanner and when to wear a feathered hat. And now she's sent me on a trip around the world to complete my education."

"Good on her," said Michael S Megabucks. "That sounds like Maria!" An idea occurred to him. "Say, ya fancy coming to meet my kid?"

Ermine looked confused. "The Duchess

never mentioned you kept baby goats."

Michael S Megabucks guffawed. "I mean my son – Mike Junior. It's his birthday today and I got something planned. You can stay over a couple of days at the apartment if you like. Mike Junior can show ya around the city."

"Oh, I'm staying much longer than that," Ermine replied brightly. "The Duchess says I can't leave until I've filled up my scrapbook. That could take weeks."

Michael S Megabucks opened his mouth to say something, then closed it again as

a thought occurred to him. As well as it being his birthday, Mike Junior had the Christmas vacation coming up and he was due to stay for a while. The kid was always asking if he could have a pet. Sure, what Mike Junior really wanted was an alligator, but a talking stoat wasn't a bad substitute.

"Great!" Michael S Megabucks grabbed his coat. "We'll be glad to have ya." He looked at the tool kit. "Is that all the luggage you got?"

Ermine shook with laughter. "Of course it isn't, silly! I mean would *you* travel the world with just a tool kit?"

"I suppose not," Michael S Megabucks admitted.

"I always carry it with me, in case there's an emergency," Ermine said. "The rest of my

16

bags are at the airport in Left Luggage."

"I'll get Sam to send someone for them straight away," said Michael S Megabucks.

Ermine jumped onto his shoulder and waved her tool kit in the direction of the door. "What are we waiting for then? Let's go and meet Mike Junior."

Ermine's whiskers twitched in excitement.
Her TRAVELS had truly begun!

Chapter 2

Meanwhile at the airport...

Two men in overcoats sat in a coffee shop in the arrivals terminal. One was short and fat with a tattoo across his knuckles and a false beard. The other was tall and slim with slicked-back hair and a pair of dark glasses. They had chosen a corner table away from other customers so they wouldn't be seen.

The tall one picked up
a discarded newspaper and
began to read.

New York Breaking News

SPUDD BROTHERS ESCAPE FROM PRISON!
Mystery of famous Toffany Diamond remains unsolved!
REWARD OFFERED FOR INFORMATION!

"You sure the cops aren't onto us?" the short one whispered.

The tall one peered out from behind his paper. Apart from a couple of routine security guards patrolling the busy concourse, the coast was clear. "Relax," he said. "No one suspects a thing." He glared at the other man. "Though you'd better put your gloves on in case anyone sees your tattoo."

"Why?" said the other.

"Because it spells your name, you idiot."

"Oh yeah. Sorry, Harry."

Barry pulled on a tiny pair of baby-pink woolly gloves. He had made them at the knitting class in prison.

"Why'd you have to choose those?" Harry snarled. "D'you want everyone looking at you?"

Barry looked hurt. "I like pink," he said. "And anyway, I ran out of wool."

"I don't see why you got that tattoo in the first place," his brother grumbled. "I mean it's pretty dumb having your name tattooed on your knuckles when you're a robber."

"The prison guard said it was a good idea," Barry protested.

"Sure he did." Harry sighed. He checked around to see if anyone was looking, put on his hat and stood up. "Now let's get that diamond back from its hiding place." He strode off in the direction of Left Luggage.

Barry hurried after him. His short legs made it difficult to keep up. "You certain it'll still be there?" he panted.

Harry patted him on the head. "Of course it'll still be there. You saw the paper. If anyone else had found the diamond, it wouldn't be a mystery any more, would it?"

The two men approached the counter cautiously. The attendant didn't look up. He was collecting a very large number of very small cases of assorted colours from the store behind the counter and piling them onto a trolley.

"Ahem," said Harry.

"Be with you in a minute," the attendant said.

Barry leaned over. "That's a lot of bags," he observed.

"Yeah, they're the property of a passenger by the name of Miss E Stoat," the attendant replied. "Flew in from Balaclavia earlier today. Someone's just come to collect them for her."

LEFT LU

"Stoat?" Barry said. "That's an unusual name."

"You could say!" The attendant chuckled. "Kinda suits her though, from what I could see."

"How come?" Barry asked. He liked chatting to people. In fact, that was how the Spudd Brothers had ended up in prison – because Barry couldn't keep his mouth shut.

"It doesn't matter!" Harry growled. Any minute now Barry would be telling the attendant his life story, including the part about them breaking out of jail and coming to the airport to retrieve a stolen diamond from Left Luggage. In fact it was only by not telling his brother anything about where the diamond was hidden until that morning that Harry had managed to keep it a secret for so long.

The attendant placed one more bag on the pile. He beckoned to the courier who was standing nearby. "Okay, that's the lot," he said. "You can take them now."

The courier disappeared with the trolley towards the exit.

"Now what can I do for you gents?" said the attendant, giving them his full attention.

"We're here to pick up a package," Harry said.

"Got a ticket?" the attendant asked.

"Yeah." Harry reached into his pocket and handed him a mouldy cloakroom ticket.

The attendant frowned. "This looks years old."

"We've been away…" Barry began.

"On holiday," said Harry quickly.

"Anywhere nice?" asked the attendant.

Barry opened his mouth to reply but Harry cut him off. "It was okay," he said. "The rooms were a bit small." He wished the attendant would stop asking questions.

"Aw, I don't know – they weren't bad for a prison," Barry said.

Harry gave his brother a kick. "He means hotel," he said. "It's just his sense of humour."

"Funny." The attendant rummaged around in the store. Then he handed Harry a small leather case with a metal clasp and a smart handle. "Here you are."

"You sure that's the one?" Harry asked, examining the case. It was so long since he'd left it there it was hard to remember exactly what it had looked like, apart from the fact it was dark blue. "Shouldn't it have a ticket?"

"This was on the floor next to it." The attendant held out a yellowing ticket stub and compared it with the one Harry had given him. "See, the number matches."

Harry examined the two tickets. It certainly seemed like it was the right case.

"Why don't you open it and check everything's there, just to be on the safe side?" the attendant suggested.

"That's a good idea, Harry," said Barry.

"No, it's not!" Harry poked him hard in the ribs with his elbow. He tucked the little case under his coat. "And my name's not Harry, it's…er… Harri-et. See you around."

He grabbed Barry's arm and pulled him in the direction of the lift.

Once inside, Harry pushed the button for the top floor of the car park.

The door opened. They made for their clapped-out old banger of a car.

"That's a good idea, Harry!" Harry mimicked as they jumped into the car and slammed the doors. "Are you a complete dope? What if he'd seen the diamond? And why did you have to tell him my name?"

"Sorry." Barry looked crestfallen. "I think you covered it pretty well though. You kind of suit Harriet." He made a grab for the case but Harry shook him off.

"It was my idea to hide it there, so I get to open it." He raised the little leather valise to his lips and kissed it. Then he wrinkled his nose and sniffed. A musky smell was coming from within.

"What's the matter?" Barry said.

"Smells like those ferrets Grandma Spudd used to keep in her knicker drawer." Harry took another sniff and shrugged. "Must be because it's been there so long." He snapped open the clasp. "Feast your eyes, brother. We're finally gonna be rich. This is our ticket to a new life."

"Yeah – Hawaii here we come!" Barry leaned over expectantly. Harry lifted the lid. Both men gasped. Inside the case was a small, feathered hat.

Chapter 3

Back in New York City...

E rmine sat on Michael S Megabucks's shoulder as they travelled along the wide avenues of Manhattan in his chauffeur-driven limousine. Occasionally they stopped so that Ermine could take a photo for her scrapbook.

Ermine felt quite awestruck by her new surroundings. She had never seen such tall buildings, or such beautiful shops, or so many people hurrying along the pavements wrapped up against the winter chill.

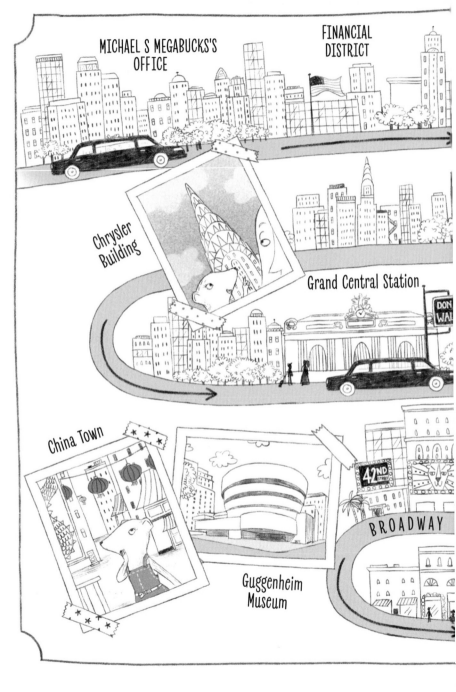

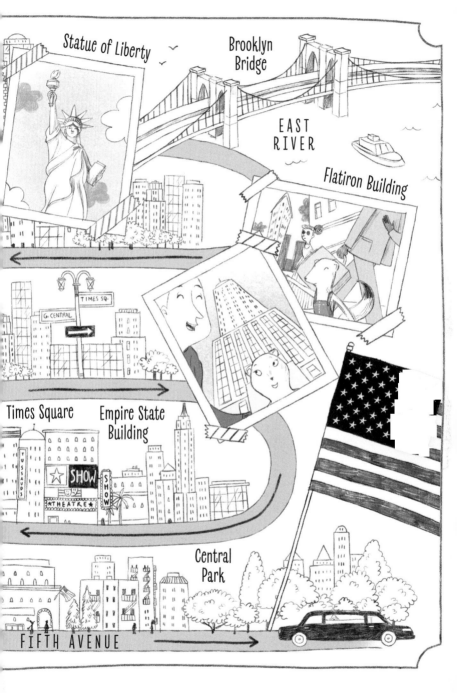

The shop windows were festooned with cut-out snowflakes, red ribbons and twinkling Christmas lights.

Bright yellow taxis honked their horns. Steam drifted from manhole covers into the crisp air.

CHIC BAGS & CO

TAXI

TAXI

MR HOT DOG

Neon signs blazed.

Ermine lowered the window and sniffed. There was a delicious sweet smell from the doughnut stalls on the street corners. Her tummy began to rumble. She couldn't wait to taste American food!

She was quite surprised when, after a little while, they came to a big, green space.

"This is Central Park," Michael S Megabucks told her.

The limo pulled up outside some wide gates.

"And this is the City Zoo."

"The zoo!" Ermine cried.

"Isn't that where you see all sorts of different animals from around the world?"

"Sure is!" Michael S Megabucks grinned.

Ermine clapped her paws in excitement. "I've read about zoos. I've always wanted to go to one!"

"Well, now's your chance!" Michael S Megabucks patted his overcoat pocket. Ermine wrapped her woolly scarf carefully around her neck, threw her camera over her shoulder, grabbed her tool kit and climbed into the pocket. The two of them got out of the car.

Just then a tall, dark-haired woman came hurrying towards them. She was wrapped up in an expensive-looking coat.

"Is that your ex-wife?" asked Ermine, with interest. The Duchess had told her the Megabucks were separated.

"Yeah, that's Susie – Mike's mom," Michael S Megabucks replied.

Behind the woman trotted a small freckled boy, holding several large balloons.

"And that's Mike Junior!"

"Dad!" the boy shouted, running over and giving Mike Senior a hug.

Michael S Megabucks ruffled the boy's hair. "Happy birthday, son!"

Susie addressed them both. "Now remember, no late nights, no fizzy drinks, no junk food and not too much TV. And no getting into trouble." She gave Mike Junior a peck on the cheek and disappeared into a taxi.

"Can we go and see the animals now?" Ermine said from her position in Michael S Megabucks's overcoat pocket.

Mike Junior noticed her for the first time. His jaw dropped. "What's with the talking weasel, Dad?"

"I'm not a weasel, I'm a stoat," Ermine said stiffly. "And my name's Ermine." Her whiskers twitched with annoyance. "Ermine's gonna be staying with us for a little while,"

Michael S Megabucks said hastily. He
didn't want the two of them getting
off on the wrong foot. "She's come all
the way from Balaclavia to see us. I thought
you guys could hang out."

"Cool!" said Mike Junior, high-fiving
Ermine's tiny paw. "Hi, Ermine!"

"Nice to meet you, Mike," said
Ermine politely.

Michael S Megabucks crossed his fingers
behind his back. Mike Junior seemed quite
taken with their visitor.

"Can I take Ermine to see the alligators?"
Mike Junior said eagerly.

"I guess so." Michael S Megabucks sighed,
placing Ermine on Mike Junior's shoulder. "You
two go on ahead. I'll buy us some popcorn."

The three of them went in
through the gates.

"This way!" Mike Junior pushed through
the crowd towards the alligator pen.

Ermine clung onto his shoulder. The zoo
was very busy. She didn't want to fall off and
get her tail trampled.

Very soon they arrived at some railings. On
the other side of the railings was a pit containing
a large pond ringed with bushes.

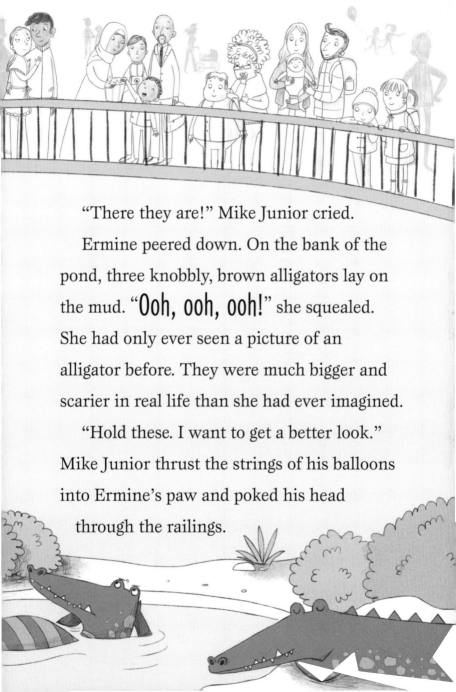

"There they are!" Mike Junior cried.

Ermine peered down. On the bank of the pond, three knobbly, brown alligators lay on the mud. "**Ooh, ooh, ooh!**" she squealed. She had only ever seen a picture of an alligator before. They were much bigger and scarier in real life than she had ever imagined.

"Hold these. I want to get a better look." Mike Junior thrust the strings of his balloons into Ermine's paw and poked his head through the railings.

Ermine suddenly felt
herself being lifted into the air.
She looked down. The ground
was getting further away.
The railings and Mike Junior
were beneath her. Ermine felt
a surge of panic. Flying was for
birds, not stoats, and she didn't
know how to get down.

"HELP!" she squeaked, but her
voice was drowned out by the
noise from the passing crowds.

Just then Michael S Megabucks
spotted the danger and shouted
from the popcorn stall.
"HEY, MIKE! WATCH OUT!
ERMINE'S FLOATING AWAY!"

Mike Junior looked up. "Don't worry, Dad. I'll get her." He made a leap for Ermine and missed.

"BE CAREFUL!" yelled Mike Senior. He started pushing his way through the crowds towards them.

"HELP!" screamed Ermine. Now the wind was sending her in the direction of the alligators. She waved her tail wildly to and fro to stop herself drifting up, up and away altogether.

Mike Junior climbed onto the railings. "Wave your tail harder," he called to Ermine.

Ermine whizzed her tail round and round like a propeller. It seemed to be slowing her down.

"MIKE, GET DOWN!" Michael S Megabucks yelled.

"I WILL ONCE
I GET ERMINE!"

Balancing shakily, Mike
Junior reached out a hand and made a
grab for Ermine. He caught hold of her
whizzing tail. "I'VE GOT HER, DAD!"

"EEK!" Ermine squeaked, just as a strong
gust of wind caught the balloons.

"OOOOAAAAAAHHHHHH!"

All of a sudden Mike Junior found himself lifted off the railings, rising a little way above the alligator pen.

"LET GO!" he shouted.

Ermine let go of the balloons.

Now she felt herself plummeting downwards at an alarming rate, with Mike Junior's fist still attached to her tail.

"OHM"

SNAP! CRA-ACK!

They both landed in the bushes.

The three alligators slid off the swampy
bank into the pond and swam lazily through
the water towards them.

Ermine glanced up. A crowd of onlookers
had gathered to see the drama unfolding.
They all looked very worried, especially a
woman in a brown
zoo uniform.

Michael S Megabucks reached the railings. The woman spoke to him quickly, then sped off. "HOLD ON, GUYS!" he shouted. "THE ZOOKEEPER'S ON HER WAY."

"Tell her to hurry up!" Ermine squeaked. The alligators were even bigger and scarier close up. Their skin was scaly and wrinkly and they had powerful-looking tails and long, flat snouts full of sharp teeth. They looked even more menacing than the foxes that used to chase her in Balaclavia when she was a kitten.

"D-d-do something, someone!" Mike Junior gulped.

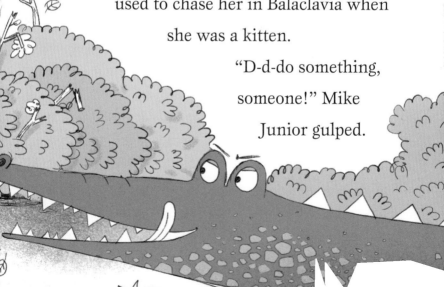

The alligators were crawling towards the bushes on their thick, stumpy legs.

Ermine wondered what to do. She'd left her tool kit in Mike Senior's pocket. Then she had a brainwave. The thought of Balaclavia had given her an idea.

She wriggled up the front of Mike Junior's shirt. "Don't worry," she hissed. "I'll distract them." Quick as a flash she took off her scarf and gave it to Mike Junior along with her camera. "Hold these," she said. Then she turned and launched herself into the air, landing right in front of the alligators.

The three creatures looked at one another and grinned wickedly. They slithered forwards, jaws open.

All of a sudden Ermine
began to fling herself about.

She tumbled...

...and flipped.

She somersaulted...

...and jumped.

She **pirouetted** and **twirled**.

She looked just like an acrobat at a circus!

The alligators halted in their tracks.

They watched, entranced.

"What are you doing?" Mike Junior whispered.

"I'm dancing, of course!" Ermine puffed. "It hypnotizes them. We do it at home, only with foxes, not alligators. It stops them trying to chase us."

Just then a metal door slid open at the back of the pen. The woman in the brown zoo uniform poked her head through.

"The zookeeper's here!" Mike whispered.

The zookeeper threw two lumps of meat to the alligators. In an instant, the animals came out of their trance and turned towards the snack, snapping at it with their great jaws.

"Quick!" the zookeeper called softly to Mike Junior and Ermine. "Over here! Run!"

Mike Junior raced out of the pen, closely followed by Ermine. She did a final backflip and with a whisk of her tail she was out.

CLANG!

The zookeeper banged the door shut behind them. "Phew!" she said. "That was close!"

Michael S Megabucks was waiting in the concrete area behind the pen. He squatted down on his heels. "That was real stupid," he told Mike Junior. "I was worried sick."

"I know, Dad." Mike Junior hung his head. "I'm sorry. I sure won't do it again."

"And no more about alligators!" Mike Senior said.

"Okay." Mike Junior's freckled face broke into a grin. "Anyway, who needs alligators? I've got Ermine." He picked her up and put her on his shoulder.

Ermine squeaked in delight. She was glad Mike Junior wasn't in too much trouble. It was his birthday after all. And he hadn't meant to fall into the alligator pen. He was just trying to save her.

Michael S Megabucks gave his son a hug. He straightened up. "There's some folks up there who want to meet you," he said to Ermine.

"Who?" Ermine said excitedly. She liked meeting new people.

"You'll see!" Mike Senior said.

The zookeeper led the way back up the steps and out onto the concourse.

The group of onlookers had swelled to a huge crowd. It now included several newspaper journalists and a TV crew who had been covering another story nearby and who had arrived just in time to film the whole rescue. When they saw Ermine everyone broke into cheers. "Ooh! Ooh! Ooh!" Ermine squealed. They were all waiting to see *her*! She wished she'd worn her feathered hat.

"Can we get an interview?" the TV
crew asked.

"Hang on a minute," Ermine said,
waving at the crowd. She turned to the
zookeeper and offered her a sweet smile.

"Could I get your picture for
my scrapbook?" she asked.
"Only the Duchess
said I had to
fill it up."

Chapter 4

On the other side of town...

Across the Hudson River in a run-down area of the Bronx, Harry Spudd was pacing the threadbare carpet of a dilapidated hotel room. The hotel was next to a railway line. Every so often a train clattered past, making the floor shake and the furniture rattle. It was a long way from the life of luxury the two brothers had been dreaming of for the last four years. In fact it was almost as bad as being in prison.

"The case must have got switched when the ticket fell off," Harry cursed.

"You mean someone else has got our diamond?" Barry said. He was lying on his back on the thin mattress, counting the cracks in the ceiling. An unpleasant smell of boiled cabbage wafted from his dirty socks.

"They must have," Harry replied bitterly. "And we got their lousy hat."

"But why haven't they come forward to claim the reward?" Barry wondered. "I mean, it's like you said, Harry – if anyone had found the diamond, it wouldn't be a mystery any more." His face creased into an ugly frown. "Unless they stole it *themselves*."

Harry stopped pacing. "Maybe…" he said, unconvinced. The sort of person who deposited feathered hats at Left Luggage didn't strike him as being the sort of person who would pilfer a large diamond. They were more likely to be the sort of sickening do-gooder who would turn the diamond over to the cops and claim the reward. And so far, it seemed that hadn't happened. But even so, Barry had a point. "Let's say someone *hasn't* stolen it," he said thoughtfully. "Let's say they took it home by mistake…"

"But why wouldn't they tell the police?" Barry said.

"Because they don't know they've got it yet!" Harry grabbed his brother by his vest and lifted him into the air so they were face to face. "That passenger – the one with all those little cases; the one who sent for her luggage – what was her name?"

"I can't remember," Barry said. "Anyway, you said it didn't matter."

"Well, it does now. Her bags were about the same size as our case – I reckon the attendant must have mixed them up and sent the diamond on with all her luggage. We need to find her so we can switch it back before she opens the case." Harry gave him a shake.

"Stop it!" Barry protested. "I can't think straight if my brains are scrambled."

Harry held him still for a minute. "Anything?" he said, thrusting his chin at his brother.

"Er…Stott…no, Scott…no, Snot…no, Spot…no…" Barry started to cry. "It's no good, I can't remember."

Harry dropped him onto the bed. He pulled

out his mobile phone. "Never mind. I'll call up Left Luggage and ask." He dialled a number. "Operator? Put me through to Left Luggage, Kennedy Airport. It's an emergency." He put the phone on loudspeaker.

BRRING BRRING! BRRING BRRING!

Hi, you've reached Left Luggage. But guess what, we've all left for the day! Please call back tomorrow or leave a message after the tone.

BEEEEEP!

Harry threw the phone down in disgust.

"Aren't you going to leave a message?" Barry asked.

"Are you crazy?" Harry shouted. "And leave a clue for the cops?" He hurled himself onto the sofa and switched on the TV.

Barry was examining the dark blue case for clues of his own. He took out the feathered hat and tried it on. "It's very *small*," he said, regarding himself in the mirror, the tiny hat perched on his head.

"Maybe it's for a doll," Harry snapped,

surfing through the channels. "Maybe she's got a pet chihuahua. Maybe she just likes small hats. Who knows? It's too late now, anyway. We're never gonna find her."

He settled on the News Channel.

Barry slumped down next to him.

A broadcast was coming live from the

City Zoo.

In breaking news, an amazing rescue took place here today when a small animal came to the aid of a boy who fell into the alligator pen. The animal, whose name is Ermine, hypnotized the alligators with a dazzling display of acrobatic dancing. Then she and the boy, who happens to be the son of one of New York's richest men – Michael S Megabucks – raced to safety with the help of the zookeeper.

"That's so cool!" said Barry. "I wonder what kind of animal did that?"

"I don't care!" growled Harry. He wracked his brains, trying to remember the conversation at the airport. **Stott, Scott, Spot, Snot** – Barry was right. It was definitely something like that.

A small white animal appeared on the screen. It had a long tail with a black tip, two coal-black eyes, white whiskers and a pink nose. It was wearing a blue pinafore dress and a woolly scarf.

"Awww, cute!" said Barry.

Harry ground his teeth. He hated animals. He hated rich people too, especially rich kids. He wished the alligators had eaten them both.

"She can talk!" Barry said in wonder. "You gotta admit, Harry, that's pretty impressive for a weasel."

"I told you, I don't CARE!" Harry growled. All he could think about was the missing diamond. If everything had gone to plan, they'd have sold it to their old pal, Dodgy Don the diamond dealer, by now. And they'd be on their way to Hawaii with ten million dollars in the bank, not watching some stupid story about a talking weasel. If only they could remember the passenger's name! He scowled furiously at the white furry figure on the screen. "Anyway, it's not a weasel, it's a stoat," he said.

Barry blinked. The word "stoat" seemed familiar somehow. "Did Grandma Spudd keep those too?" he asked.

"Only round her neck," Harry said. "They make good fur collars, stoats."

"Oh," said Barry. The word rattled round his brain. **Stoat. Stoat. STOAT.** He'd heard it recently, he was sure.

Tell us, Ermine, how did you manage to hypnotize the alligators?

Oh, that! It's what I do with foxes back home. It stops them trying to chase us. We're very clever like that, us stoats...

"See?" said Harry, interrupting the reporter. "What did I tell you? It's not a weasel, it's a stoat."

STOAT. Stoat. <u>STOAT.</u> Suddenly Barry let out a triumphant cry.

"Ohhhh YEAAAAAHHHHH!!"

"What's up with you?" asked Harry.

"That was the name of the passenger – the one with all the bags."

"What was?"

"Stoat!" said Barry. "Not Stott or Scott or Snot or Spot. S.T.O.T.E. Stoat. I remember now."

Harry sat up. "Are you sure?"

"Yes, that was definitely her name – Miss E Stoat."

Miss E Stoat?! Harry looked hard at the screen. Ermine was waving at the cheering crowds. His eyes narrowed. "Hang on a minute, didn't she say she just arrived in New York?"

"What, you mean *that*'s her?" Barry gasped. "The one what took our diamond?"

68

"**Shhhhhhh!**" Harry leaned forwards
and turned up the TV.

The Duchess?

Yes, she rescued me from the Duke when I was a baby. He wanted to use my fur to trim the collar of his robe. She lives in Balaclavia. She's the one who taught me how to use a spanner and when to wear a feathered hat...

The two villains stared at one another. Then they stared at the feathered hat. Then they stared at Ermine on the television. "**IT IS HER!!!!**" Barry cried.

"Good work, bro!" Harry gave him a pat on the head. He rubbed his hands together gleefully. "Now all we've got to do is break into Michael S Megabucks's apartment tonight and get our diamond back."

Later that night...

E rmine tossed and turned. Try as she might,
she couldn't sleep. She was in the guest
room of Michael S Megabucks's penthouse
apartment on Fifth Avenue, overlooking
Central Park. The enormous feather bed was
the most comfortable she had ever been in,
but the constant buzz of traffic from the street
below and the excitement of the day meant she
still felt wide awake. That, and the smell of the
delicious leftover pizza that was sitting in the
kitchen in a large cardboard box.

Ermine had never eaten pizza before
tonight. Now she felt she could eat it for ever.
She had already made up some interesting
toppings of her own, with the help of the chef
from *Toni Balloni's*, the local pizzeria.

Cheese and cherries

Spicy beef and blueberries

American hot and honey

Pumpkin and popcorn

Ermine's whiskers twitched at the thought. It was no good – the smell of the pizza seemed to be calling to her. She decided to sneak along to the kitchen and have a slice. She could do some work on her scrapbook at the same time!

She wriggled out of bed and pulled her dressing gown on over her pyjamas. Then she tiptoed across the thick carpet to the closet where her bags lay in neat, colourful rows. Packed inside them was everything a world-travelling stoat could need. Blue was for hats, pink was for clothes, yellow was for undies and green was for coats. (Of course, Ermine didn't need shoes most of the time, because she had two perfectly good pairs of paws.)

She thought for a moment about unpacking – there hadn't been time so far, and she wanted to take her prized feathered hat out. But then she decided it could wait until morning. Her scrapbook was in the kitchen. All she really needed was glue and scissors. So she picked up her tool kit and crept out of the door.

Ermine pattered along the dimly lit corridor past the other bedrooms. Sounds of snoring – one loud, one soft – told her that the two Mikes were fast asleep.

ZZZZZZ ZZZZ... ZZZZZZZ...

When she reached the hallway she paused. Propped up beside the front door was a brand-new skateboard. The skateboard was a birthday present for Mike Junior from his dad, but because of the adventure at the zoo he hadn't been able to try it out yet.

Ermine longed to have a go. Mike Junior had promised her a turn in the morning, but now she was up she didn't think she could wait until then. Besides which, if she practised a bit *now*, then she'd be able to do it properly when they went to the park tomorrow. She was sure Mike Junior wouldn't mind.

Ermine scurried over. She lowered the skateboard gently to the floor, hopped on and pushed herself off with her back paw.

WHOOSH!

Ermine felt the wind in her ears. This was easy! And almost as much fun as the tobogganing she did in the winter back in Balaclavia!

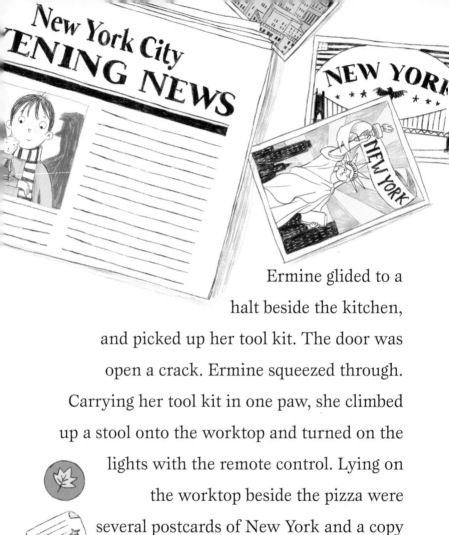

Ermine glided to a halt beside the kitchen, and picked up her tool kit. The door was open a crack. Ermine squeezed through. Carrying her tool kit in one paw, she climbed up a stool onto the worktop and turned on the lights with the remote control. Lying on the worktop beside the pizza were several postcards of New York and a copy of the *Evening News*, waiting to be cut out and pasted into her scrapbook.

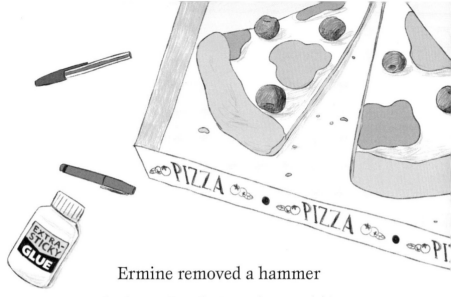

Ermine removed a hammer
and a box of nails from her tool kit so
she could reach the items underneath and
laid out everything she would need:

○	EXTRA-STICKY glue	☑
	Scissors	☑
	Stickers	☑
○	Pens	☑

She helped herself to a slice of cheese-and-
cherry pizza and set to work on the scrapbook.

Very soon she had created a lovely collage.

She finished it off with a few stickers. Then
she sat back on the stool to admire her work.

SPLAT!
CRASH!

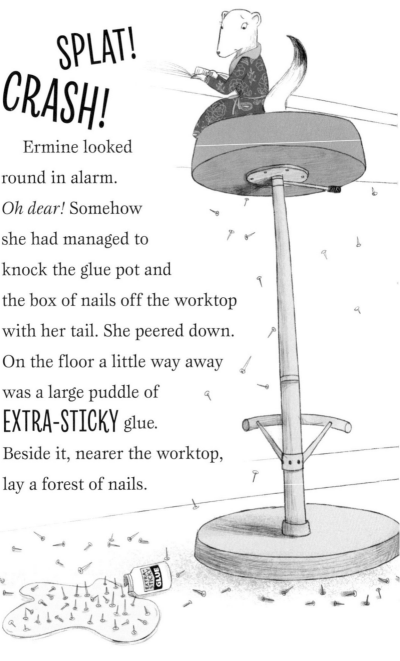

Ermine looked
round in alarm.
Oh dear! Somehow
she had managed to
knock the glue pot and
the box of nails off the worktop
with her tail. She peered down.
On the floor a little way away
was a large puddle of
EXTRA-STICKY glue.
Beside it, nearer the worktop,
lay a forest of nails.

Ermine wasn't sure what to do. She didn't
know where to find a mop or a broom, and
she definitely didn't want to risk getting her
tail stuck in the glue. It would be better to
clear it up in the morning when the glue was
dry. She hoped Mike Senior wouldn't mind.
He probably got up early to go to work and
he might not be very pleased when he saw
the mess in the kitchen…especially if the
cleaning up made him late.

Suddenly Ermine had a brainwave.
She would make Mike Senior breakfast
to say sorry for the mess, and make
sure he got to work on time.

She opened a cupboard to see
what she could find.

Cola
Fizzymints
X-TRA STRONG chilli sauce
Hot dogs
Buns

Ermine removed the items one by one and arranged them carefully on the worktop. She stroked her whiskers thoughtfully. Normally she had boiled eggs and soldiers for breakfast, and she didn't really know what any of this strange American food was, but if it tasted as good as pizza, it would be just fine!

She arranged the hot dogs on a plate with the buns. After some hesitation, she decided the **X-TRA STRONG** chilli sauce must be there to cool the hot dogs down.

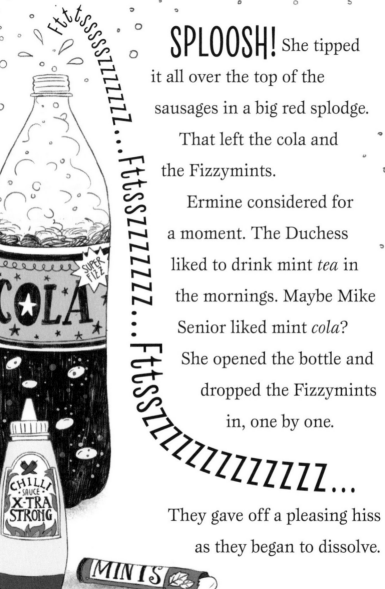

SPLOOSH! She tipped it all over the top of the sausages in a big red splodge. That left the cola and the Fizzymints.

Ermine considered for a moment. The Duchess liked to drink mint *tea* in the mornings. Maybe Mike Senior liked mint *cola*? She opened the bottle and dropped the Fizzymints in, one by one.

They gave off a pleasing hiss as they began to dissolve.

Suddenly Ermine let out a gigantic

YAWN.

She felt like she'd been hit with a brick. It had to be the jet lag catching up with her at last. The Duchess had warned her it would.

Ermine screwed the cap back on the cola bottle wearily. Then she collected her tool kit, turned off the lights, picked her way carefully around the mess and headed back out of the kitchen to bed. She was fast asleep almost before her head touched the pillow.

Chapter 6

A little while later...

The kitchen window of Michael Megabucks's mega-apartment flew open. Harry Spudd leaped nimbly through it. He was dressed in dark clothes and a balaclava, with the hat box tucked into his pocket. Barry's fat form squeezed painfully after him and collapsed beside the sink.

"Tell me again, why couldn't we take the lift?" he groaned. The two brothers had climbed up the side of the huge apartment block using a rope and a grapple hook.

"Because someone might have seen us, you dope!" Harry hissed. "Now, come on."

Barry looked round fearfully. The kitchen was pitch-black apart from a thin finger of light coming from the doorway. "Can't we turn the lights on?" he whispered. "You know I'm afraid of the dark."

"No." Harry cuffed him on the head. "Use the torch."

Barry switched on his torch. A thin beam of light wobbled round the kitchen. It fell on the worktop where Ermine had laid out breakfast.

"Food!" Barry breathed. He was starving.

The climb up the rope was more exercise than he'd done in the last four years put together. He tugged on Harry's sleeve. "Can I have some? Before we start looking for the diamond?"

"No."

"Aw, please, Harry. Otherwise my tummy might rumble and wake everyone up."

"Oh, all right then," Harry agreed.

Barry's tummy sounded somewhere between a volcano and an angry bear when it rumbled. It was a nasty trait Barry had inherited from Grandma Spudd. "Hurry up! And go easy on the cola – we don't want you burping."

Barry's burps were even worse than his rumbling tummy. It was another nasty trait he'd inherited from Grandma Spudd. (There was a third, but it's too rude to tell you about.)

"Okay." Barry tiptoed towards the worktop. Suddenly he stopped dead.

"What's the matter?" Harry hissed.

"My feet are stuck."

"Don't be daft."

Barry pulled with all his might. "They are, Harry, honest." He held out his arms like a scarecrow.

Harry marched over. Then he stopped dead too. His shoes felt as though they'd been glued to the tiles. "What the…?"

"See?" Barry said.

"I told you."

"Take your shoes off. We'll step over it."
Harry pulled one foot out of his shoe and
took a giant stride forward. Then he pulled
the other foot out of the other shoe and took
a second giant stride forward. He beckoned
to his brother. "It's fine over here."

"Okay." Barry made to follow.
Unfortunately for him, his stride was much
shorter than his brother's. Barry opened his
mouth to scream.

"YEEEEOOOOOWWWWW!"

ap!" Harry hissed sharply.

e up the whole apartment! What's the

matter with you anyway?"

Barry's face went from red to purple. "I

think I trod on some tacks," he gasped.

Harry shone the torch on the floor. "You're

right," he said. The area where Barry was

standing was covered in nails. Behind that

were two puddles of glue with two pairs of

shoes stuck in the middle of them. Harry

narrowed his eyes. "Someone's laid a trap," he

muttered. He picked up Ermine's scrapbook

and touched it gingerly with one finger. The

glue was still wet. "Looks like it was the

stoat," he said, examining the scrapbook.

"You think she's onto us?" Barry grunted

"I don't see how she could be. Maybe it's

just a weird habit stoats have. Like guarding
their territory or something. Now get over here."

Barry picked his way through the nails in

his socks.

"Shhhhhhhhh!"

Barry reached the worktop. "Hot dogs!" he said, rubbing his hands together in delight. "With ketchup! My favourite."

"Wait…" Harry began. There was something funny about the ketchup. It looked a bit lumpy. "Maybe you should stick with the cold pizza."

But the first hot dog was already on its way into Barry's mouth. Barry bit down on the bun and chewed.

"YEEEEOOOOWWWWW!"

This time his face turned from red to purple to blue and back to red. He coughed and spluttered.

Harry slapped him hard on the back.

"What's the matter now?"

"Hot...hot...hot...hot...hot..." Barry grabbed the bottle of cola and unscrewed the cap. Brown liquid frothed out. He raised the bottle to his burning lips.

"Wait..." Harry began again. The cola seemed awfully fizzy considering no one had shaken the bottle. And it smelled strongly of mints.

Barry ignored him. He took a long drink of cola. "Phew," he said, flapping at his mouth with his free hand. "That's better." He finished the bottle.

Harry picked up the discarded Fizzymint wrapper. He frowned. "Hey, Barry, remember when we were kids and Grandma Spudd used to make those cola bombs in the garden?"

"Yeah," Barry chuckled. Grandma Spudd's cola bombs were legendary. They had more power than your average jet-propelled rocket. "What about it?"

"What did she put in them to make the cola explode?"

"Fizzymints," said Barry. "Why?" He flashed the beam of his torch onto Harry's face. It wore a horrified look. "What's the matter?" asked Barry. Just then, he noticed a strange feeling in his gut. He looked down. His stomach was expanding at an alarming rate, as if someone was blowing it up with an air pump.

"I think I've got a burp coming," Barry said, his stomach churning. "You might want to shut your ears." He opened his mouth.

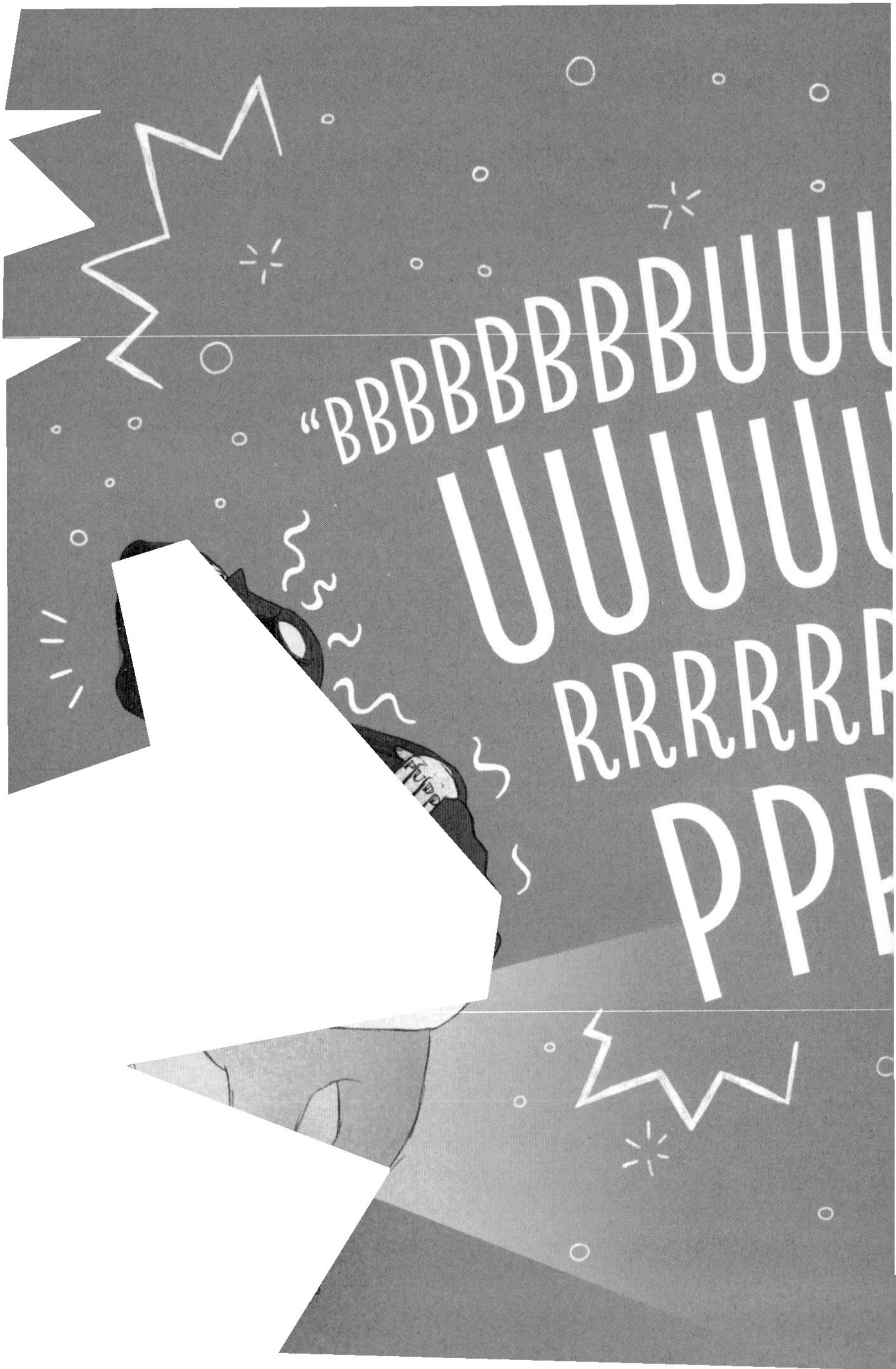
“BBBBBBBBUUU
UUUUU
RRRRRR
PPP

UUUUU
RRRRRRRRRR
RRPPPPPPP
PPPPPPPPPPPPP!!"

The burp was so powerful it lifted Barry off his feet. It was so gassy it set off the smoke alarm.

BEEP-BEEP-BEEP-BEEP-BEEP!

The two villains heard the sound of a door opening down the corridor.

"Who's there?" a man's voice shouted.

"It's Megabucks!" Harry hissed. "Let's get out of here before he sees us. We'll take the lift." He made for the kitchen door.

"Okay." Barry raced after him.

Harry rushed into the hall.

"**YEOW!**" He tripped over the skateboard and landed face down on top of it.

"**OOOOPPPPHHHHH!**"
Barry toppled onto his brother, squashing him flat.

The skateboard surged forward. It shot across the hall and down the corridor past Mike Senior, who was coming the other way.

Mike Junior emerged from his bedroom. "What's going on, Dad? "We've got burglars!" Mike Senior shouted. "They're making a getaway. Look out!" Mike Junior jumped out of the way. The skateboard was picking up speed. Sparks flew from its wheels as it whizzed over the shiny floor.

"Make it stop!" shouted Barry.

Harry tried to use his toes to brake.

"I can't!" he screamed.

At the end of the corridor was a large picture window, which looked over Central Park. The skateboard hurtled towards it.

The two Mikes watched helplessly.

CRASH!

The glass shattered. The skateboard sailed out into the night sky, the Spudd brothers still on top of it. At that moment a noise erupted from Barry's bottom accompanied by an unpleasant smell. (I think you know what it was, but it's still too rude to mention.)

THHHFFFFFFFFFFFFFFTTTT

"Wow!" Mike Junior ran to the window holding his nose, and stared out. For a moment the two villains were silhouetted against the moon...

Then they disappeared from view.

From somewhere in the distance came a faint **splash**.

"Do you think they'll be all right, Dad?" Mike Junior said.

Mike Senior clapped a hand on his son's shoulder. "Yeah. As long as they can swim, that is. Sounds like they landed in Central Park Lake! Let's call the cops and tell them to pick 'em up." He steered his son towards the kitchen.

Mike Junior whistled. "I had no idea that skateboard was so fast, Dad."

"Neither did I." Mike Senior stopped abruptly. "Hang on a minute, what was it doing outside the kitchen anyway? I thought I put it by the front door."

The two Mikes looked at one another.

Ermine!

They started to laugh.

"Say, where *is* Ermine?" Mike Junior wondered.

"I'm here!" A small, white, furry face poked round the spare-room door wearing a cross expression. "I wish you'd stop making such a racket," Ermine complained. "I was trying to get some sleep!" She wrinkled her nose. "And what is that awful smell?"

Chapter 7

The next morning...

"All I did was try out the skateboard and make Mike Senior some breakfast," Ermine explained to the police officer.

They were in the kitchen at the apartment. The police officer (or "cop" as Mike Junior called her) was taking statements from everyone about the break-in, while another officer took photographs of the crime scene. A caretaker was busy boarding up the hole in the window at the end of the corridor.

"What about the shoes?" The police officer pointed to the two pairs of shoes glued to the floor.

"I knocked over the glue pot when I was filling up my scrapbook," Ermine told her. "It was the **EXTRA-STICKY** variety," she added. "I suppose they must have trodden in it."

"The **EXTRA-STICKY** variety…" The police officer wrote it down. Then she leaned over and sniffed the half-eaten hot dog. Her eyes watered from the heat of the chilli sauce. "You made that?" she asked.

"Yes! I told you. It was for Mike Senior's breakfast. I wanted to make up for the mess."

Michael S Megabucks raised an eyebrow. Even a drop of **X-TRA STRONG** chilli sauce was enough to burn holes in the roof of your mouth, and it looked as if Ermine had used the whole bottle. He was glad the burglars had eaten it, not him.

"I used all the chilli sauce to cool down the hot dogs," Ermine explained.

"That's not what it does," Mike Junior said. "Chilli sauce makes food really, really spicy, especially if it's X-TRA STRONG!"

"Oh!" said Ermine. Honestly, there was so much to learn when you went on a world trip!

The police officer closed her notebook. "Well, Miss Ermine, I must say you sure set a good burglar trap!" She bent down, cut round the shoes with a penknife (avoiding the tacks) and levered them carefully off the floor. Then she placed the cola bottle and the Fizzymint wrapper into a plastic container for fingerprinting later. "What about this?" she said, holding it out to Ermine.

"It's mint cola," Ermine explained. "I put

109

the Fizzymints in to give it some flavour."

"Mint cola?!" the police officer guffawed. "Are you kidding me?"

Ermine shook her head. "No, I promise. The Duchess drinks mint tea, you see, so I thought Mike Senior might like mint cola."

Mike Junior regarded Ermine with awe. "You made a *cola* bomb? *For real?*"

"A cola bomb?" Ermine looked horrified. "I don't know – did I?"

Michael S Megabucks thought he'd better explain. "See, Ermine, if you add Fizzymints to cola, it creates a chemical reaction. After a while, it explodes."

"Oh," said Ermine. "Well I suppose I must have done then."

Everyone collapsed in fits of laughter.

"Those burglars must have got one heck of a shock!" Mike Senior hooted.

"I wish I could have seen their faces when they realized what it was." Mike Junior chortled.

"No wonder they skateboarded out of the window!" the other officer roared.

Ermine felt her whiskers twitching. She could see the funny side now. She really *had* set a burglar trap, even if she hadn't meant to!

"We'll take these down to forensics for testing," the second officer said, his voice serious again, "but if you ask me, this is the work of the Spudd Brothers. Pity we didn't manage to pick 'em up last night but there was no sign of 'em when we got to the lake."

"The Spudd Brothers?" Mike Junior echoed. "You mean the diamond thieves? The ones who just escaped from prison?"

The officer nodded. "They fit the description you and your dad gave. One tall and thin; the other short and fat."

"But why burgle us?" Michael S Megabucks asked.

The police officer shrugged. "I guess they just fancied breaking into a nice apartment to see what they could find to tide them over."

"You mean you don't think they've got hold of the missing diamond yet?" Mike Junior asked.

"I don't see how they could have," the police officer said. "Or, like your dad said, why would they burgle you?"

"What missing diamond?" Ermine said, intrigued. This was turning into quite an adventure.

"A few years back the Spudd Brothers stole the world's biggest diamond from Toffany's, the famous jeweller's on Fifth Avenue," the officer told her. "They were arrested and sent to prison for the robbery, but no one ever found out where they hid the diamond. Or at least, no one came forward with it to claim the reward."

"Reward?" Ermine squeaked. "What reward?"

"Whoever helps recover the diamond gets $10,000 and the opportunity to try on anything they want in the Toffany's store."

"That sounds wonderful," sighed Ermine. She loved trying on jewellery – and she could put the photos in her scrapbook to show the Duchess! Plus $10,000 would go a long way towards mending the Duke and Duchess's leaky roof...

"Well, one small problem – *we* don't know

where the diamond is and the Spudd Brothers do," Mike Junior reminded them.

The police officer nodded. "You're right, I'm afraid. The thieves must be planning to pick up the diamond as soon as they can and make their getaway. It's our job to find them before they do. Anyway, we'd best be going." He raised his cap to Ermine. "It's been a pleasure meeting you, Miss."

"Can I have your photo for my scrapbook?" Ermine asked. "The Duchess said I had to fill it up."

"Sure." The officer posed for a photo with Ermine.

"And if you ever want a job at the NYPD, give us a call." The two officers let themselves out.

Michael S Megabucks looked at his watch. "Shoot. I'd better go too – I'm late for a meeting. How about I meet ya later at the Rockefeller Centre? You can show Ermine the sights. I'll send the limo to pick you up," he told Mike Junior.

"Okay, thanks, Dad."

Michael S Megabucks threw on his coat and strode after the police officers.

"What's the Rockefeller Centre?" Ermine asked.

"It's where they have the huge Christmas tree," Mike explained. "It's got everything – shops, restaurants, a famous theatre.

It's even got an ice-
skating rink…"

Ermine clapped
her paws together
in delight. "I love
ice skating!" she cried.
"And I've got the perfect
outfit for it. It matches my
white fur." She scampered
off across the hall. "I'll go
and get ready."

Back in her room, Ermine
selected a pink suitcase from the closet and
laid the contents on the bed, along with the
other things she would need for her outing.

She quickly changed out of her pyjamas
into her skating outfit.

"Let's get the elevator to the Top of the Rock first and see the view," Mike Junior suggested from outside the door. "Dad's got VIP tickets. We can go anytime we like."

"Should I wear my feathered hat?" Ermine asked. The Top of the Rock sounded rather posh. She retrieved the little dark-blue case from the closet and opened the catch.

"No," Mike Junior called back. "It's seventy floors up. It might get blown off."

Ermine snapped the catch back into place. She felt disappointed. She'd been looking forward to wearing her feathered hat. She rammed the skating boots into her tool kit, wrapped her woolly scarf round her neck and threw her camera over her shoulder.

Just then the intercom buzzed.

"The limo's here," Mike Junior shouted.

Ermine grabbed her tool kit. She eyed the dark-blue case longingly. She really *did* want to wear her feathered hat.

"Hurry up!"

She could always wear it when she went skating… Ermine picked up the little blue valise in the other paw and hurried out of the apartment after Mike Junior.

Chapter 8

Outside the apartment block...

H arry and Barry Spudd sat shivering inside their clapped-out car, keeping watch. They were both in a foul mood. The car heater didn't work properly, they had no shoes, and their clothes were still damp from when they'd landed in Central Park Lake. They were also very tired and extremely hungry – without the diamond, they were broke.

"This is all your fault," Harry grumbled.

"I don't see how," Barry countered, removing a cheesy sock and examining his sore foot.

"You were the one who burped, remember?"

"Yeah, and you were the one who tripped

over the skateboard."

"Don't remind me," Harry glowered. He pressed his aching back against the car seat. He felt a lot *flatter* than the previous day since Barry landed on top of him.

"Anyway, now what?" Barry asked.

Harry patted his pocket, which contained the case with Ermine's feathered hat in it. "We'll wait until the kid and the stoat go out, then sneak into Megabucks's apartment and switch the cases."

"I'm not climbing up that rope again," Barry said, putting his sock back on.

"We'll find some other way," Harry said. He trained the binoculars on the apartment building.

Just then Ermine emerged jauntily through

the front doors. Clutched in one paw was a dark-blue leather case.

"Curses!" Harry spat. "She's got the diamond with her! We've got to catch her before she does anything with it."

Ermine and Mike Junior gave the doorman a wave and stepped into a sleek black limo.

Harry turned the ignition.

The engine coughed into life. The two villains pulled out after the limo.

"Don't lose them!" Barry said.

"Don't worry, I won't!" Harry replied.

BEEP! BEEP! BEEP!

The battered old car dodged through the traffic after the limo. They whizzed along Fifth Avenue past Toffany's. The sight of the dazzling diamonds in the windows made them more determined than ever.

After a little while, the limo drew to a halt outside the Rockefeller Centre. Mike Junior emerged with Ermine sitting comfortably on his shoulder, the blue case in one paw.

"They're heading for the Top of the Rock," Barry said, clambering into the backseat to get a better look.

The car screeched to a stop. The Spudd brothers jumped out and slammed the doors. They hurried across the road and entered the building. Inside, crowds of people were milling about in the reception area, admiring a huge glass chandelier. Everything was decked out in fairy lights and tinsel, ready for Christmas.

"Over there!"

At the other end of the reception area was the elevator hall. Ermine and Mike Junior were stepping into the one in the middle with an attendant.

Harry set off in pursuit, pulling his brother after him.

"Shouldn't we get a ticket?" Barry asked anxiously.

"We don't have time for that," Harry snapped. "Hurry up or we'll lose them."

The two villains rushed forwards.

A uniformed lift operator barred their way. He regarded them coldly. "Tickets, please."

"I told you we needed a ticket, Harry!" Barry said. He blinked, realizing what he'd said. "I mean, er, Harri-*et*!"

Harry went red. "How much?" he snapped.

The lift operator pointed to the lift with Ermine in it. "Sixty-five dollars each for VIP, or thirty-two dollars each to join the queue." He gestured to a long line of people that snaked backwards and forwards across the hall.

"That's daylight robbery," Harry complained. He pulled a crumpled ten-dollar note from his pocket. "That's all we've got."

"Then you'll have to take the stairs," the
lift operator said snootily.

1,215 stairs and quite some time later, the villains arrived at the observation deck.

Barry staggered out onto the platform and collapsed.

"Get up, you loser!" Harry said.

"I can't!" Barry moaned. Climbing the stairs to the Top of the Rock was more exercise than he'd done in his whole entire life! He didn't think he'd ever be able to walk again.

Harry gave him a weak kick. "Pull yourself together or you won't be going to Hawaii. Find the stoat."

"Okay, okay!" Barry rolled over and sat up. He pulled the binoculars from his pocket and searched the deck. Suddenly he let out a sob. Tears rolled down his cheeks.

"What's the matter with you now?"

Barry held out the binoculars and pointed mutely.

"For ferrets' sake!" Harry exclaimed, putting the binoculars to his eyes. Ermine and Mike Junior were getting back into the VIP lift to go down! The little blue case was still swinging from Ermine's paw. Harry growled. His face set in a furious expression. "There's no way some stupid stoat's getting away with our diamond. Come with me." He grabbed his brother by the arm.

"Where are we going this time?" Barry groaned.

"To catch that lift."

"But how?"

"You'll see."

They headed for a door. Attached to it was a large sign, which read:

⚠ DANGER
VIP LIFT SHAFT
DO NOT ENTER

"You sure about this, Harry?" Barry said anxiously.

"Shut up." Harry unpicked the lock and pushed the door open. The two men slipped in.

"This way." Harry raced down the narrow passageway. "Hurry up!"

They rounded a corner.

The passageway ended in a narrow platform. Below that was a huge square void full of cables. And disappearing down it at considerable speed was the VIP elevator.

"We'll have to jump!" Harry cried.

"I c-c-c-c-c-can't," Barry stammered. "I'm scared of heights."

"Too bad." Harry gave his brother a shove and leaped after him.

"WHOOAOOAOOAOO

The two of them landed with a thud on
the top of the elevator. It rocked slightly, then
ground to a shuddering halt.

Chapter 9

Inside the VIP elevator...

"What's the matter?" asked Mike Junior.

"I'm not sure," the lift attendant said, pressing the controls. He frowned.
"It felt like something landed on the roof."

"Like what?" Mike Junior asked.

"Maybe it's a very large pigeon," Ermine suggested.

The lift attendant shrugged. "Whatever it was it seems to have jammed the system. It's programmed to shut the whole lot down if anything happens." He sighed. "I guess we'll just have to wait for the engineer to fix it."

"No, we won't," Ermine contradicted him. "I can do it. That's why I carry my tool kit," she explained, "in case there's an emergency." She rummaged in the bag and selected a tiny screwdriver and a pair of pliers. Then she climbed up Mike Junior and perched on his shoulder. It was just the right height for her to reach the control panel.

"What are you going to do?" Mike Junior asked her.

"Override the system, of course," Ermine said impatiently. *Honestly,* she thought, *humans could be awfully slow!* She removed the metal faceplate with the screwdriver, her face a picture of concentration. "Here," she said, handing the faceplate to the attendant.

"Are you sure you know what you're doing, Miss?" the attendant asked anxiously. The wiring looked very complicated.

Ermine fixed him with a steely stare. "Of course I know what I'm doing – the Duchess taught me."

"Don't worry," Mike Junior told him. "Ermine can do pretty much anything if she puts her mind to it."

Ermine picked up the tiny pliers with her other paw. Very delicately, using the screwdriver and the pliers in her front paws, she rewired the controls.

"That should do it." She screwed the faceplate back on. "Try now."

The attendant pressed the button. This time it worked! The elevator shot towards the bottom.

"I told you she could do it!" Mike Junior grinned.

Ermine felt pleased. All the things the Duchess had taught her back in Balaclavia were proving to be very useful on her travels. Suddenly her sharp ears heard a noise. A high-pitched wailing seemed to be coming from somewhere above them.

"What was that?" she said.

"What was what?" asked Mike Junior.

"I thought I heard a scream."

The attendant shrugged. "Must have been

the wind," he said. "It whistles past when we go at full speed."

"What is full speed?" Ermine asked with interest.

The elevator's progress through the building was displayed on a screen. She hadn't really paid it much attention on the way up because she'd been so excited to see the view, but now she regarded it with intense curiosity.

"WHOAOO!;"

They seemed to be hurtling down like lightning.

"365 metres per minute," said the lift attendant. "It takes forty-two seconds to complete the ride."

"Cool!" Mike Junior said.

"No wonder it sounds like someone's screaming!"

"Yeah. It doesn't normally last this long though," the attendant said, as the noise continued. "I'll get it checked out."

The lift reached ground level. Ermine and Mike Junior waved goodbye to the attendant and made their way to the ice-skating rink.

"Ooh, ooh, ooh!" squealed Ermine. The rink was sunk into the middle of the Rockefeller Centre, surrounded by glamorous shops and tall buildings. On one side was a beautiful golden statue rising out of a stone pond. Behind it was the tallest, bushiest Christmas tree Ermine had ever seen, even counting the forests back home in Balaclavia. It was dripping with thousands of different coloured lights, which shone like enormous jewels. On the other side of the rink, steps led down to a viewing platform where lots of people were taking photographs. There was a lovely holiday atmosphere.

"I need to change into my skating boots,"

Ermine told Mike Junior. "And my feathered hat!" She was so glad she'd brought it.

"Okay, I'll get some milkshakes. What flavour do you want?"

"Pinenut?" Ermine suggested. She'd never had a milkshake before and wasn't sure what flavours were available.

"I don't think they have that," Mike Junior said. "How about strawberry?"

"All right." Ermine scuttled off to the locker room, clutching her two bags.

She removed her skates from the tool kit ready to put them on, threw off her scarf and rushed over to the mirror to check her outfit. The soft white velvet dress matched her winter fur perfectly. All she needed now was her feathered hat!

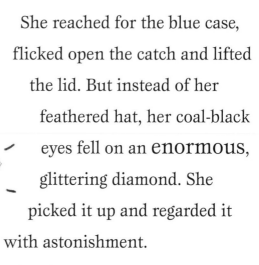

She reached for the blue case, flicked open the catch and lifted the lid. But instead of her feathered hat, her coal-black eyes fell on an enormous, glittering diamond. She picked it up and regarded it with astonishment.

Just then the door to the locker room flew open.

Two men stood framed in the doorway – one tall and thin and flat-looking, the other small and fat. They both had very white faces and their hair stood straight up from their heads as if they'd seen a ghost. Neither of them was wearing shoes.

Ermine blinked at them. They looked

extremely cross,
although she couldn't
for the life of her think
why. Then she remembered
what the police officer had
said about the diamond and the
two thieves who had escaped
from prison. She gasped.

The Spudd Brothers!

"Looking for this, were you?"
Harry panted, opening
a small blue case.

Ermine regarded
the contents of
the case with
amazement.

Her feathered hat!

"Because we've been looking for *that*." Harry pointed at the diamond. "We hid it in Left Luggage. The cases got switched at the airport."

So that was what happened!

"Only you wouldn't just let us switch them back when we broke into the apartment, would you?" Barry said menacingly. "You decided to give us the runaround."

"I didn't *mean* to," Ermine said indignantly. "It's not my fault you skateboarded out of the window into Central Park Lake."

"How about the chilli dogs? And the cola bombs? And making us climb all the way to the Top of the Rock and risk our lives on the way back down again?" Harry hissed.

"Yeah, didn't you hear me screaming?" Barry put in. His hands trembled.

144

"I don't know how I wasn't sick."

"Oh, that was *you*!" Ermine said. It all made sense now. That was why the lift stopped – the villains must have jumped on top of it. And the noise they'd heard inside the elevator really *was* someone screaming. No wonder the Spudd Brothers looked as if they'd seen a ghost!

Still, thought Ermine crossly, *it wasn't her fault – it was theirs!* The black tip of her tail twitched in annoyance. "You can't blame *me*," she said. "You shouldn't have stolen the diamond from Toffany's in the first place."

"Yeah, well we did. And now we're gonna take back what's ours…" said Harry.

"…and make *you* into a pair of earmuffs," Barry chortled.

Harry dropped the case containing the

feathered hat and kicked it out of the way.

"Mind my hat!" Ermine squeaked.

"Stuff your hat," said Harry.

"Yeah, and stuff you!" added Barry.

The two villains advanced on Ermine.

"Hey, you clowns! Pick on someone your own size!"

It was Mike Junior! He stood in the doorway, clutching two giant strawberry milkshakes.

The villains rounded on him. "Get out of our way, kid!" Harry snarled.

"Or what?" Mike Junior held up the milkshakes. "Quick, Ermine, run!"

Still clutching the diamond in one paw,

Ermine slung her skates over one shoulder,

dodged past the Spudd Brothers and scampered out of the locker room.

"Have these on me, losers!" Mike Junior cried. He hurled the milkshakes at the robbers.

SPLOOSH!

The villains found themselves covered from head to toe with chilled pink milkshake. "She's getting away!" Harry spluttered, wiping a squashed strawberry from his eyes.

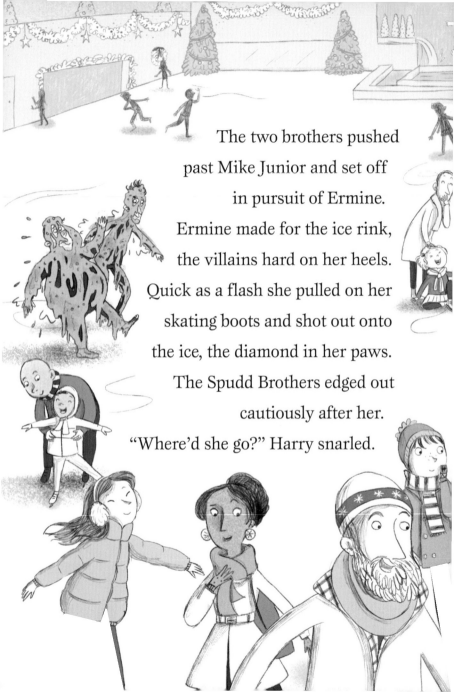

The two brothers pushed
past Mike Junior and set off
in pursuit of Ermine.
Ermine made for the ice rink,
the villains hard on her heels.
Quick as a flash she pulled on her
skating boots and shot out onto
the ice, the diamond in her paws.
The Spudd Brothers edged out
cautiously after her.
"Where'd she go?" Harry snarled.

"Search me! I can't see her anywhere."
Barry wheezed, clinging onto his brother.

Ermine had almost completely
disappeared. Thanks to her white winter
coat and matching skating outfit, she and
the diamond were practically invisible
against the sparkling ice.

Only one little bit of her gave her
away, and the villains were far too
preoccupied to notice what that was.
(I bet you can guess though.)

"I'm f-f-f-f-f-freezing!" Harry stuttered.

"M-m-m-me t-t-t-t-too!" Barry shivered, his lips blue.

"I c-c-c-can't move!"

"M-m-m-me n-n-n-n-neither!"

The combination of having no shoes, wearing damp clothes and being doused in strawberry milkshake was having an unfortunate effect on the Spudd Brothers. The ice rink was making them freeze from the socks up!

They ground to a halt in front of the magnificent Christmas tree, frozen solid.

"Yoo-hoo!" Ermine's voice floated up from the rink.

Mike Junior skated over. He looked hard at the ice.

SWISH, SWISH, SWISH.

A black furry arrow shot this way and that. Mike Junior grinned. It was the tip of Ermine's tail! He bent down and picked her up.

"Good work!" Ermine sat in Mike Junior's cupped hands, her skating boots dangling over his thumb.

"Here, this is yours." Mike Junior pulled her feathered hat out of his pocket.

"At last!" said Ermine, planting it firmly on her head.

Then she gave the villains a winning smile. "You don't mind if I get a photo for my scrapbook, do you?" she said. "Only the Duchess said I had to fill it up."

Dear Duchess,

I am having an amazing time in New York. I have made great friends with Michael S Megabucks and Mike Junior (especially since I stopped him being eaten by an alligator on his birthday). They've asked me to stay for Christmas! I have already been to lots of exciting places, like the Rockefeller Centre, where I fixed the elevator and went ice skating. While we were there Mike Junior and I caught two robbers and recovered the missing Toffany diamond they stole before they went to prison. (The police had to come and defrost them before they were arrested, but that's another story.)

Today we're off to Toffany's to claim the reward. Mike Senior says you should have the $10,000 to fix your roof, which I think is a brilliant idea. And I get to try on all the jewellery I want! I am keeping my scrapbook up-to-date so I can show you all my photos when I get back. And don't worry - I'll make sure I get a really good one at Toffany's.

Merry Christmas!

Lots of love, **Ermine**

PS: Please could you write and tell me where I'm going next on my travels? I think I fancy somewhere hot.

Grand Duchess

Maria Von Schnitzel

The Imperial House of Hasbeen

Hasbeen Castle

Balaclavia

Europe

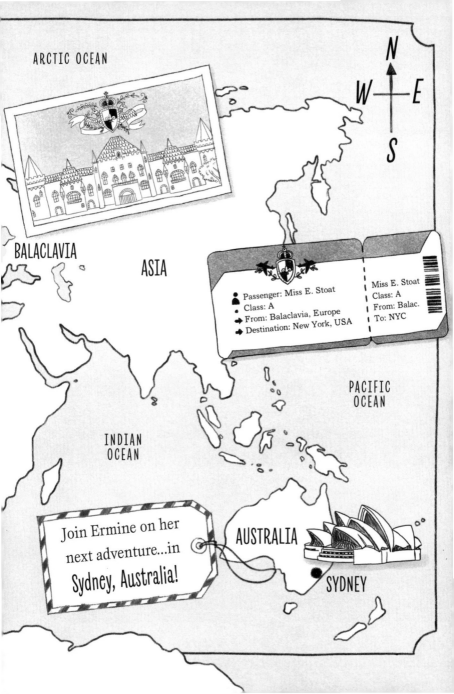

How to make a trav<

Ermine loves sticking photos, tickets, maps, postcards and more in her scrapbook as a way of remembering all the fabulous places she's visited. Why not give it a go yourself?

MY SCRAPBOOK

Step 1: Choose your scrapbook

Choosing the right scrapbook is very important. Think about how big you want it to be, what you might want on the cover, and what sort of paper you'd like.

Ermine's top tip:
I love the smell of a new scrapbook, and I even chose a shiny ribbon to go around mine!

Step 2: Find your memories

Once you've found your scrapbook, it's time to start collecting. You can put anything in a travel scrapbook. Tickets? Check! Photos? Check! A leaf from a park you've visited? Check!

scrapbook like Ermine

Step 3: Stick it down

Now you're happy with the layout of your page, it's time to start glueing!

Ermine's top tip:
I always leave my pages to dry out before closing my scrapbook.

NEW YORK

very big TEETH!

Ermine's top tip:
I always place everything on the page first, so I can move things around and make sure I'm happy with how it looks!

Step 4: Travel!

Decide where you want to travel to next...

Ermine's top tip:
I love to explore – from new countries and cities, to my own home, the outdoors, indoors and anywhere else I fancy. All you need is a dash of determination, a sprinkle of courage, and a dollop of curiosity!

Happy travels!

To Shaheena,
who loves animals,
books and travel
Jennifer

To all readers, little and big,
who face their life with
wonder, curiosity and a hint
of imagination Elisa

First published in the UK in 2018 by Usborne Publishing Ltd., Usborne House,
83-85 Saffron Hill, London EC1N 8RT, England. www.usborne.com

Text copyright © Jennifer Gray, 2018
The right of Jennifer Gray to be identified as the author of this work has been
asserted by her in accordance with the Copyright, Designs and Patents Act, 1988.

Illustrations copyright © Usborne Publishing Ltd., 2018
Illustrations by Elisa Paganelli.

The name Usborne and the devices ♀♁ are Trade Marks of Usborne Publishing Ltd.

A CIP catalogue record for this book is available from the British Library.

JFMAMJJAS ND/17

ISBN 9781474927253   04333/1
Printed in China.